A LITTLE
CHRISTMAS
TREE

To Fred and Robyn, for instilling in me a love of stories
To Mimi and Nicole, for letting me tell them stories
To Amy, Addison and Mackenzie, for letting me be a part of their story

And to Kent and Kay, for inspiring the ending to THIS story

First Edition
Printed in China. First Printing: 2017
www.printninja.com

ISBN 978-0-692-91244-7

A LITTLE CHRISTMAS TREE

WRITTEN BY ANTHONY MERRILL & MICHAEL BAST
ILLUSTRATED BY DAN BURR

Deep within a glen, tucked up against a scraggy mountain lived Little Tree, a small Scotch Pine. His shape was perfect and his branches full.

"Little Tree, you are beautiful, and one day, for one special family, you will bring the true meaning of Christmas," said his momma.

Little Tree glowed inside for this was his greatest wish. More than anything, he wanted to be a Christmas tree. From the time he was a sapling, he heard wondrous stories of Christmas. The birds, who nested in his branches, told him of the sparkling lights, the tinkling bells, and the towering star decorating each tree.

Every year, when the air became cold and snow blanketed the forest, the lumberjacks came to harvest new trees for Christmas. Little Tree would extend his branches and tiptoe to the sky, hoping he would be chosen.

"Too short," one lumberjack said.

"Too skinny," another complained.

Each year Christmas would come. And each year Little Tree was left behind.

"Is there something wrong with me, Momma?" Little Tree asked.

"Of course not, sweetheart. Be patient. One day, to one special family, you will bring the true meaning of Christmas. Wait and see."

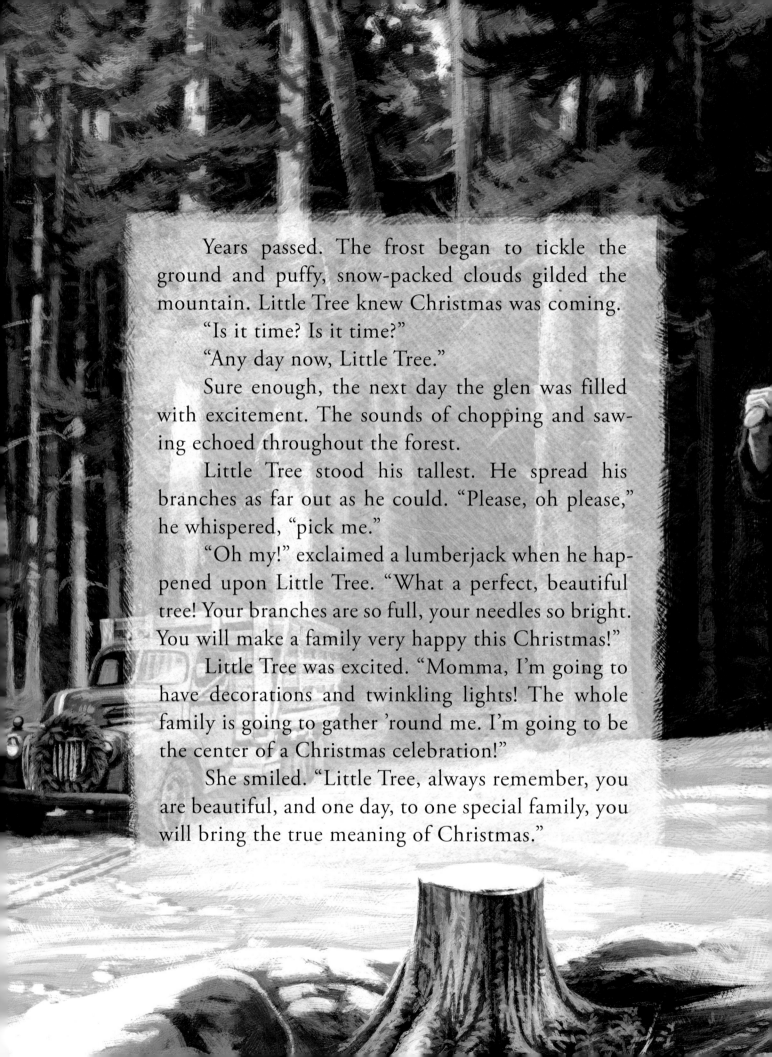

Years passed. The frost began to tickle the ground and puffy, snow-packed clouds gilded the mountain. Little Tree knew Christmas was coming.

"Is it time? Is it time?"

"Any day now, Little Tree."

Sure enough, the next day the glen was filled with excitement. The sounds of chopping and sawing echoed throughout the forest.

Little Tree stood his tallest. He spread his branches as far out as he could. "Please, oh please," he whispered, "pick me."

"Oh my!" exclaimed a lumberjack when he happened upon Little Tree. "What a perfect, beautiful tree! Your branches are so full, your needles so bright. You will make a family very happy this Christmas!"

Little Tree was excited. "Momma, I'm going to have decorations and twinkling lights! The whole family is going to gather 'round me. I'm going to be the center of a Christmas celebration!"

She smiled. "Little Tree, always remember, you are beautiful, and one day, to one special family, you will bring the true meaning of Christmas."

The lumberjack cradled Little Tree in his arms and carried him to his old truck. He loaded him up with the other trees and fastened them down with thick ropes. The truck let out a rusty cough and sparked to life. All the trees beamed, delighted to be headed down into town for Christmas.

But the old road was icy and filled with potholes. As the truck crept down the mountain, the jostling shook Little Tree free from the ropes. He slid until one of his branches got stuck against the side of the truck. The old truck hit a jagged stone. There was a jolt, and then...

SNAP!

Little Tree's biggest branch splintered in two.

Eventually the truck reached the tree lot. The trees were unloaded and presented for inspection. The owner of the tree lot walked over to them. Little Tree immediately caught his eye.

"What a perfect tree! You'll sell fast!" he said. But then he saw Little Tree's broken branch. He frowned and walked away. "What a shame. He would have fetched top dollar."

"Do you want us to get rid of him, boss?" his assistant asked.

The owner rubbed his chin. "No, let's put him in the front of the lot for everyone to see."

"But why, boss? He's busted."

"Not from this side he isn't," he said, spinning Little Tree around. "People will see how perfect he is from the road and hurry in to buy him up."

Little Tree was placed in front of the lot underneath a bright lamp for all to see.

He was so happy. From where he was standing all of Main Street spread out before him.

As night fell the town burst into color and activity.

Little Tree couldn't believe it. Christmas was even better than the birds' stories!

"Will you look at that one!" said a man surrounded by children, pointing at Little Tree. "He's a beauty."

Little Tree's needles bristled with excitement. This was going to be his family. He just knew it.

"Can we get him? Can we get him?" one little girl asked excitedly.

As the man circled around Little Tree, his face fell. "Oh, not this one. He's broken. We can find a better tree. Come on, kids, I think I saw a pretty one over here."

Little Tree was confused. He had stood up tall. He had spread his branches wide. He didn't understand. Why wasn't he chosen?

Only a few minutes later, another family came. They rushed toward him. They looked him over, but they, too, moved on and picked a different tree.

Despite his disappointment, Little Tree's excitement and hope remained. "This is the night. I know it! A family is going to choose me, and I will help bring them the true meaning of Christmas!"

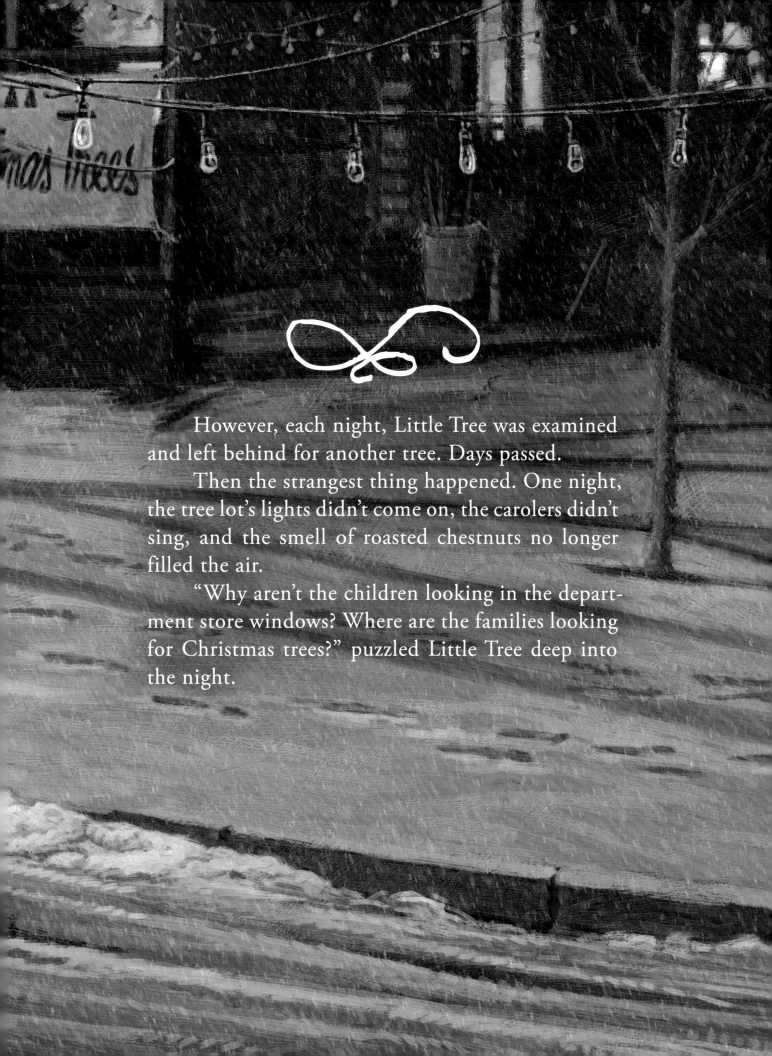

However, each night, Little Tree was examined and left behind for another tree. Days passed.

Then the strangest thing happened. One night, the tree lot's lights didn't come on, the carolers didn't sing, and the smell of roasted chestnuts no longer filled the air.

"Why aren't the children looking in the department store windows? Where are the families looking for Christmas trees?" puzzled Little Tree deep into the night.

The next morning, a muddy truck backed up next to him. The lot owner lumbered over to Little Tree. "Well, you served your purpose." He was heaved into the truck.

He wondered why he was being treated so roughly. But as the truck began to roll out of the lot, Little Tree's confusion turned to excitement.

"I'm going to the lot owner's home! I've been chosen! I'm going to be his Christmas tree!"

He started to imagine the lights that would be strung across his branches and the star that would adorn his highest perch.

All my dreams are coming true, he thought. *My momma was right! I'm going to bring the true meaning of Christmas to a family . . . my family!*

The truck skidded to a stop. Little Tree was dragged out and thrown onto the ground. The truck disappeared into the distance.

Little Tree looked around. There was junk everywhere. A faded sign high above him spelled out:

CITY DUMP!

Little Tree had been thrown away.

Time passed. Gradually his bright needles turned brown and fell off. His full branches began to wither and curl. The weather slowly warmed until the summer sun beat down on him. He could feel his bark peeling away and his trunk becoming tough and stiff.

Alone in the garbage dump, Little Tree often wondered what he had done wrong. Then one day he felt it. The north wind blasted across him, and he knew Christmas was coming. While he lay there thinking about the lights and carolers he wouldn't ever see again, an old man trudged through the garbage toward him.

The old man kneeled down next to Little Tree and ran his hands over his branches. After a moment he exclaimed, "You'll work perfectly!"

He lifted Little Tree over his shoulder and carried him out of the dump. Little Tree was placed in a small sleigh pulled by two dogs, reminding him of the wolves that lived in the forest.

The forest, the glen, and Momma, Little Tree thought. It seemed so long ago and distant from where he was now. As they approached the man's cabin, Little Tree saw the warm orange glow of a fireplace.

He sighed. "Well, at least I'll be able to keep him warm this Christmas."

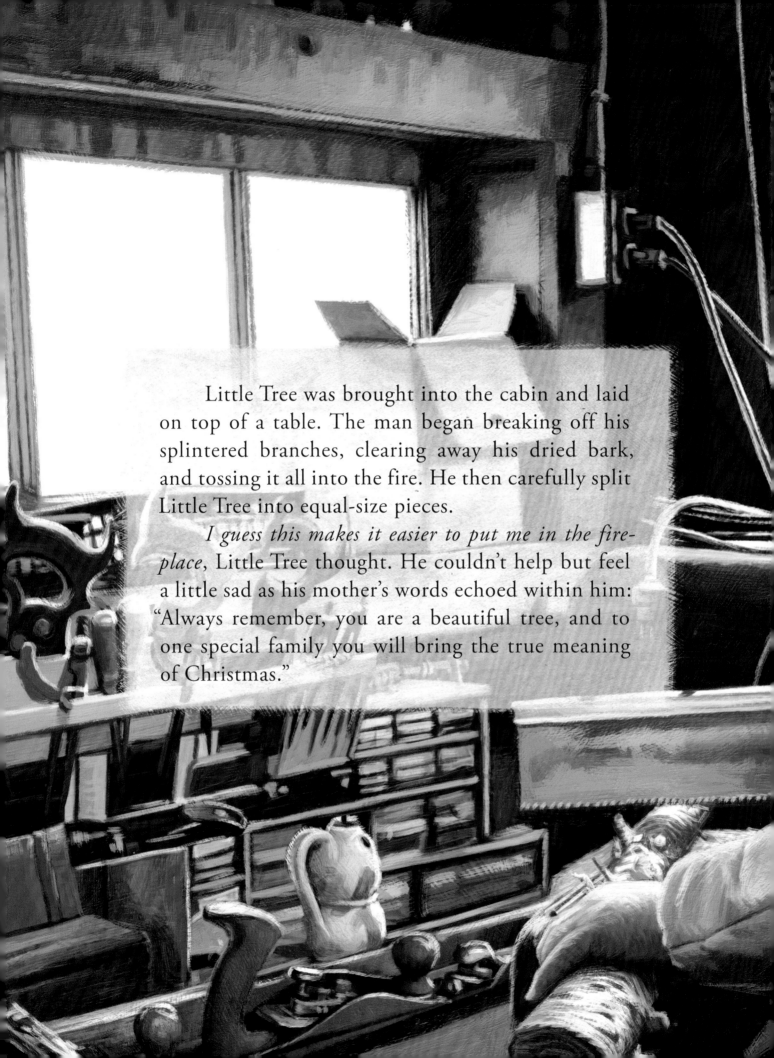

Little Tree was brought into the cabin and laid on top of a table. The man began breaking off his splintered branches, clearing away his dried bark, and tossing it all into the fire. He then carefully split Little Tree into equal-size pieces.

I guess this makes it easier to put me in the fireplace, Little Tree thought. He couldn't help but feel a little sad as his mother's words echoed within him: "Always remember, you are a beautiful tree, and to one special family you will bring the true meaning of Christmas."

Little Tree waited to be thrown into the fire. But the man pulled a knife from his back pocket. His hands moved slowly and carefully. He worked on each piece of Little Tree, carving a part here, notching the wood there. This went on for many days. After carving, he took sand paper and rounded off the corners and smoothed over the wood. Then he massaged them in warm oil until they glowed with a soft, shiny luster. He lovingly wrapped each piece and placed them in a big box.

Little Tree felt a gentle jostle as the box was lifted. He heard the motor of a car and the vibration as it rumbled down the road, reminding him of the bumpy ride down the mountain that felt so long ago.

After a short time passed, the car came to a stop. He could hear the sound of thick boots crunching through the fresh snow, and with each step the sound of singing became louder. There was a knock on a door and then an explosion of sound.

"Grandpa!" a little girl squealed.

"Hello, sweetheart," the old man said.

"Is that for me?" she asked.

Little Tree felt the box change hands.

"What is it, Grandpa?"

"You'll have to open it to find out."

The girl opened the box and pulled out the first wrapped gift. She tore away the paper and found an expertly carved lamb.

"Wow!" she exclaimed. "It's so beautiful!"

Little Tree glowed inside. "She likes me!"

She opened each piece revealing more small animals, until she came to a carving of a man clad in long robes and wearing a crown.

"Who is this?" she asked.

"He was a king," the old man said.

"Why is he kneeling if he is a king?"

The old man smiled. "Keep opening."

Little Tree was as excited as the girl, wondering what was coming next.

She opened the next present and gasped. "It's Baby Jesus!" She turned and hugged her grandfather.

"You're right. And who was he?"

"Our Savior—and the true meaning of Christmas."

Little Tree's heart soared. He had done it.

Every year when the air turns cold and the snow begins to fall, Little Tree is placed in the center of the mantle where he can hear the singing, see the sparkling lights, and smell the rich fragrance of the season. And every year, into the heart of his new home, Little Tree brings the true meaning of Christmas.